Camp-out

Story by
Joyce Maynard

Pictures by
Steve Bethel

Harcourt Brace Jovanovich, Publishers   **HBJ**   San Diego   New York   London

During his work on this book, the artist was supported in part by
an Individual Artist's Grant from the New Hampshire Commission on the Arts
and the National Endowment for the Arts.

Library of Congress Cataloging in Publication Data
Maynard, Joyce, 1953—
Camp-out.
Summary: A family goes on an overnight camp-out
where they cook over a campfire, swim, and sleep
in sleeping bags.
1. Children's stories, American. [1. Camping—
Fiction] I. Bethel, Steve, ill. II. Title.
PZ7.M4716Cam 1985   [E]   85-5504
ISBN 0-15-214077-8

Printed in the United States of America
First edition   A B C D E

The paintings in this book were done in acrylic on Monadnock paper.
The text type was set on The Linotron 202 in ITC Cheltenham Light. The
display type was filmset in Cheltenham Ultra. Color separations were
made by Heinz Weber, Inc., Los Angeles, California. Composition by
Central Graphics, San Diego, California. Printed by Rae Publishing Co.,
Inc., Cedar Grove, New Jersey. Bound by A. Horowitz & Sons, Fairfield,
New Jersey. Designed by Joy Chu.

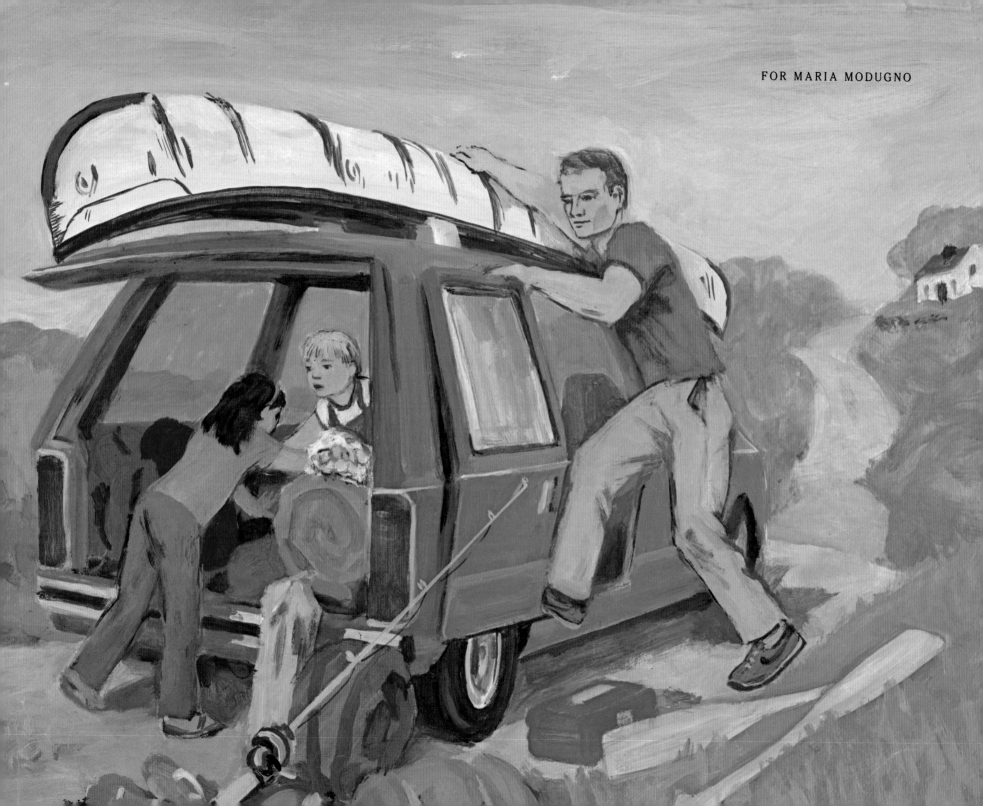

FOR MARIA MODUGNO

"We're going to sleep outside tonight," Audrey told Charlie.
"It's called a camp-out. We're going to Big Bear Island."

"Will there be bears?" asked Charlie. "Can I bring my sword?"

"No bears," said Audrey.

"Will my bed be outside?" asked Charlie.

"We get to sleep in sleeping bags," Audrey explained.
"Even Baby Willy."

"It's not bedtime yet," said Charlie. "I just had lunch."

"Later," said Audrey. "You'll see."

The family drove for a long time. Dad started singing "This Land Is Your Land."

"Know what, Dad?" said Audrey. "This highway *does* look like a ribbon."

"This road looks like a snake," said Charlie. "I'm going to eat you up. GRRR!"

"Snakes don't growl, Char," said Audrey. She pointed a finger at his head and made circles in the air. "You're a nut," she said.

"I'm a boy," said Charlie. "I'm a big boy."

Their friends Desmond and Tyson and their dad, George, were already at the lake when the family arrived. Tyson was wading in the water looking for frogs. "I just missed catching a big one," he called out.

"What a relief," said Audrey.

The birchbark canoe with Dad and Desmond and Charlie headed out first for Big Bear Island. Then George and Audrey followed in the green canoe, and Mom and Tyson and Willy trailed behind in the red one. A grown-up sat in the back of each canoe, to steer.

Audrey had to keep switching her paddle from side to side because her arms got tired. Up ahead, Desmond and Dad were counting their strokes. "One, two, three." Dip, row, back. "One, two, three." Dip, row, back.

They heard something go "WhooWHOOwhoo."

"A loon," said George. He cupped his hands around his mouth and made a noise that sounded almost the same. The loon dived underwater.

Dad and Desmond were already unloading the gear from the birchbark canoe when the others reached the island. "I wonder what happened to the pinecone man I left here last year," said Audrey.

Charlie was running back and forth along the path from the shore to the campsite as the sun slipped lower in the sky.

"Does everybody have a job to do?" asked George.

"We'll put up the tent."

"We'll get firewood."
"Me too."

"I'll build the fire."

"I'll wrap the potatoes in foil and make hamburgers."

Sizzle. Pop. Crackle.

"Let's eat."

After dinner the kids got two marshmallows apiece. One of Audrey's fell off her stick into the fire. Everyone watched it puff up big and then crinkle away to ashes. Charlie rubbed his eyes.

"Time to sleep," said Mom, giving Charlie his bear.

Mom led Charlie to the tent. "When you're camping," she explained, "you don't wear pajamas to bed, just the clothes you have on."

It was cold away from the campfire. She took off his shoes and set them just outside the tent. She snuggled him in his sleeping bag.

"Audrey and Tyson and Desmond will come along soon," said Mom. "And Willy and the grown-ups will be sleeping nearby."

Then Charlie was alone, looking
at the ceiling of the tent. Outside,
wind rustled the leaves. "Mommy,"
he cried, "there's trees in my tent.
MOMMY!"

Audrey ran into the tent to comfort her brother. Mom followed closely behind.

"Those are shadows," Audrey told him. Mom sang him his favorite song, "The Fox Went Out on a Chilly Night," and the other children came to listen. Desmond made a fox shadow on the side of the tent with his fingers.

Then Dad crawled inside the tent. "Guess what's in my hand," he said.

"An M&M?" asked Audrey hopefully.

"Nope," said Dad, uncurling his fingers to show a little green light. "It's a glowworm," he said. "It can be your night-light."

It was dark everywhere. The water lapped against the shore. Crickets sang. One loon called to another. Then the sun came up.

Desmond jumped out of his sleeping bag and ran out of the tent. The ground was wet with dew.

"Where's Willy?" asked Charlie.

"Let's go catch frogs," said Tyson.

"Too early," Audrey groaned, burrowing down in her sleeping bag.

"Come on," said Desmond. "You too."

George was building up the campfire, and Dad was making fishing poles for Charlie and Audrey.

"Let's see if you have some pee," said Mom, leading Charlie to a spot behind some bushes. "Then we can go for a swim."

Audrey took charge of breakfast. "You measure the pancake mix," she told Desmond, "and I'll break the eggs."

Tyson poured in the milk. Desmond dumped in the blueberries.

Audrey plopped batter on the griddle. Tyson was in charge of flipping.

They named each pancake according to what it looked like. One was Boot. Another was Jellyfish. Another was Dump Truck.

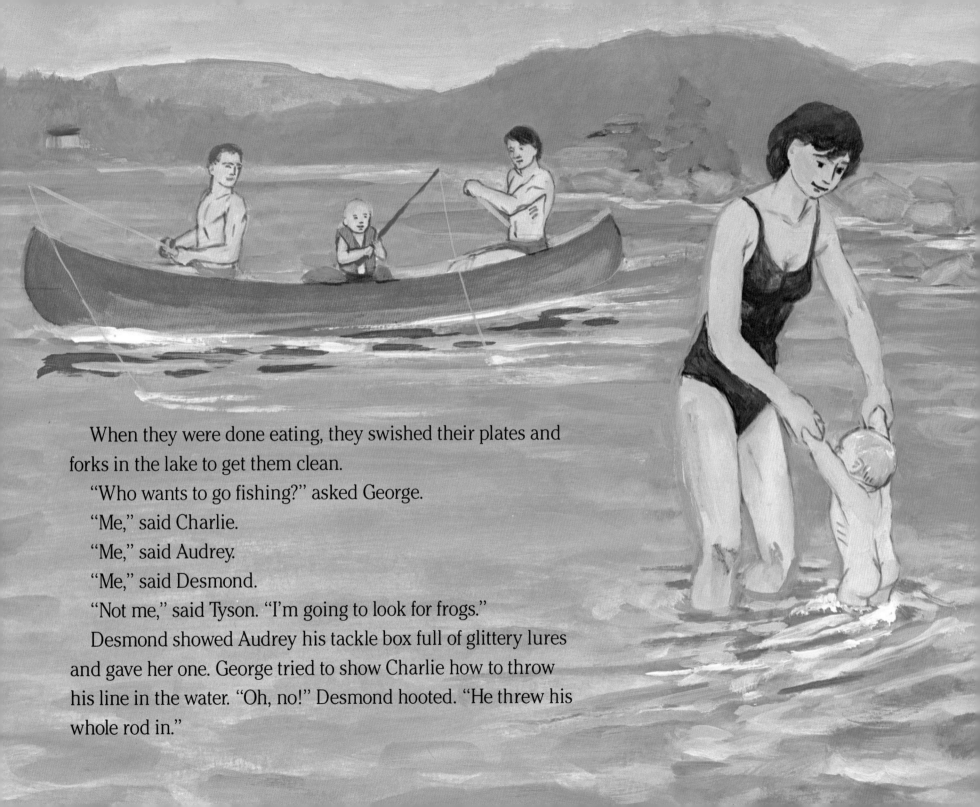

When they were done eating, they swished their plates and forks in the lake to get them clean.

"Who wants to go fishing?" asked George.

"Me," said Charlie.

"Me," said Audrey.

"Me," said Desmond.

"Not me," said Tyson. "I'm going to look for frogs."

Desmond showed Audrey his tackle box full of glittery lures and gave her one. George tried to show Charlie how to throw his line in the water. "Oh, no!" Desmond hooted. "He threw his whole rod in."

Audrey found an odd-shaped rock. "Watch this," said George.
He threw it on a bigger rock, breaking it to pieces.
"Arrowheads!" said Desmond.
"I'm going to bury one," said Audrey. "To dig up next summer."

Then it was time to pack up and head back across the lake. Everyone helped carry the tent, knapsacks, picnic baskets, sleeping bags, and garbage to the beach. Dad poured a potful of water on the coals to make sure the fire was out. It sizzled and smoked. He took one last look around the campsite and bent down to pick up Willy. "Don't worry," he said. "We would never forget you."

Paddling away from Big Bear Island, they saw motorboats bringing families to shore, all dressed up for church. Mom and Audrey, in the green canoe this time, sang "White Coral Bells" and "Amazing Grace" while Charlie dozed. Desmond and Dad were up ahead again, counting strokes. "One, two, three." Dip, row, back. A loon called. George and Tyson answered.

Their blue car and George's red truck were waiting by the shore. The men beached the canoes. Tyson took off after frogs again. Desmond and Audrey fed some ducks that had followed them back to shore.

Charlie woke up. "Time to get out of the boat, camper boy," said Mom.

"But I don't want to go home," said Charlie, starting to cry.

Just then George came out from a wooded spot near the truck. "If everyone's very helpful packing up the cars," he said, "I'll show you an Amazing Nature Surprise."

He led them into a clearing and pointed at a dead tree. "Look. The surprise."

There, attached to a limb, was something orange and bumpy and speckled and ruffly.

"It's monster brains!"

"It's alive! I saw it move!"

"Eeee-uck. What is it?"

"A mushroom or fungus of some sort," said George.

Tyson reached out to touch it.

"Don't!" Audrey yelled. "It could be poisonous. Remember what happened to the elephant that ate the polka-dot mushroom in *Babar*."

"Audrey's right," said George. "Just look, don't touch. We'll leave it for other campers to find."

"Time to go," said Mom.

But first Dad lined everybody up next to the fungus tree to take a picture. "I'll set the timer so I can be in the picture, too," said Dad. He put the camera on a rock and pushed a button. The camera started ticking. Then Dad scrambled back and found a spot next to Mom.

"Everybody make a noise like a loon," said Mom.

"WhooWHOOwhoo!" Even Willy joined in. The camera went click.

"Can we come back next summer?"

"Absolutely."